To Fran

So glad you li

the snaps.

Charlie Watts

LANDSCAPE IN FRANCE

BETWEEN LE PONT DE MONTVERT AND FLORAC, LANGUEDOC

CHARLIE WAITE

LANDSCAPE IN FRANCE

TEXT BY A. N. WILSON

ELM TREE BOOKS · LONDON

ELM TREE BOOKS
Penguin Books Ltd, 27 Wrights Lane, London W8 5TZ (Publishing & Editorial)
and Harmondsworth, Middlesex, England (Distribution & Warehouse)
Viking Penguin Inc., 40 West 23rd Street, New York, New York 10010, U.S.A.
Penguin Books Australia Ltd, Ringwood, Victoria, Australia
Penguin Books Canada Limited, 2801 John Street,Markham, Ontario, Canada L3R 1B4
Penguin Books (N.Z.) Ltd, 182-190 Wairau Road, Auckland 10, New Zealand

First published in Great Britain 1987 by
Elm Tree Books

British Library Cataloguing-in-Publication Data
Waite, Charlie
Landscape in France.
1. France—Description and travel—1975—
—Views
I. Title II. Wilson, A.N.
914.4'04838'0222 DC20
ISBN 0-241-12130-2

Printed in Spain by
Cayfosa Industria Gráfica, Barcelona

I should like to thank Caroline Taggart,
Kyle Cathie and Peter Campbell for their
constant enthusiasm, and Richard Binns for his guidance.
The French road engineers,
past and present, for the finest road network
in the world. Also Mozart and Santana for their respective
musical company.

I should also like to dedicate all the
photographs in this book to Lorna as an expression
of my eternal gratitude.

CHARLIE WAITE

NEAR CHINON, LOIRE

LANDSCAPE IN FRANCE

The movement of waters after the Ice Age, and the thunderous transformation wrought by volcanic eruptions made the world as we see it: rocks, mountains, plains, valleys, hills. When looking at extraordinary rock formations – as it were the snow-clad peaks of L'Aiguille du Dru near Chamonix, or the vast gorges of the Auvergne or the strange pink porous boulders on the northern coast of Brittany – I find it comforting to think that they came there as a result of a mighty upheaval of the earth, a movement which at the time would have seemed (had any observer then existed) wholly destructive. Likewise we may believe when, by some act of folly or chance, life has been obliterated from the face of the earth, the land will still be there. And though for the first few ages of the post-nuclear apocalypse the scene be barren as the moon, life will almost certainly return. Blades of grass will once more be seen in the crevices of the rocks. Waters will move, and in the waters, creatures. Nature is stronger than we are.

It is not surprising therefore that thoughtful people have always been awestruck by the land. Nor may we wonder that peoples have been shaped, in their destiny and character, by the land in which their ancestors struggled into existence. We are not surprised to find that men and women born in fertile, sun-soaked wine – or olive – growing regions of the Mediterranean are completely different from Northerners who live in cold lands where little grows and where there is grain but no grape. A history could be written on the effects of alcohol on the destiny of nations. Men drunk on vodka or whisky behave differently from those drunk on the wines of Burgundy.

The chief glories of France are comestible and potable, so that for many of us the geography of France reads more like a menu than an atlas. Almost any journey in France – from Brie to Lyons, from Lorraine to Camembert – sounds more like a meal than a peregrination as we step like figures in some surreal glutton's fantasy from cheese to sauce, from flan to entrée. Even at Crécy we are not sure if we are standing on a battlefield or commemorating a soup. And this Land of Cockayne, fat with food, runs with rivers of wine,

"O fortunate Burgundy, whose breasts produce so good a milk!" Many a traveller must have echoed Erasmus's words when driving, or better still cycling, through the gentle landscape of Burgundy, where every name on a sign-post reads like something from a wine-seller's catalogue: Chambertin, Vougeot, Nuits St Georges, Beaune, Pommard, Meursault, Montrachet . . . Very often a name which, from its illustrious reputation on a label has achieved legendary status, turns out to be a tiny estate, a small chateau, something little more than a farm. The best time to be there inevitably, is at the time of the *vendange*, the grape harvest, in the middle of September or thereabouts. Throughout the summer, the wine-growers have been watching the weather with utmost anxiety. If there is too little rain, the grapes will not swell, but if there is too much they will be spoilt by mildew and lose their *bouquet*. A worse possibility is that the crop will be altogether destroyed by hail or violent storms. So many things can go wrong. Perhaps that is why the celebrations at the *vendange* are so happy, when the grapes are gathered in, and the almost miraculous process of their transformation has begun. None of the arts of man is more dependent on the land, and on the munificence of Nature than wine-making. And though not the most dramatic, Burgundy is one of the most beautiful parts of France. I think of the country north-west of Beaune, rising to the rolling pastoral landscape of the Plateau de Langres. Northwards still, and the hills roll gradually away past Avallon to Auxerre and Sens in the valley of the river which gives its name to that department. There is a marvellous road from Sens to Auxerre, following the banks of the Yonne through lush meadows and past groves of tall, shimmering poplars which thrive in the deep wet soil of that valley. There one feels the force of those lines in *Henry V*, spoken by Burgundy, about

> this best garden of the world
> Our fertile France.

But it is not only in their wines that the variety and subtlety of the French genius consists. Those who love the French must be outraged by any attempt to generalise about their national character. And yet the strength of that character is so overwhelming that one cannot blame foreigners who try to explain it or chronicle it. Out of France have come the most delicious tastes ever to beguile the human palate; some of the most disturbing ideas ever to excite the human mind (Pascal, Voltaire) as well as some of the silliest (Céline, Sartre). And if France did not give birth to the most fascinating of all the great political monster-geniuses, then it raised him from the dignity of corporal to the grandeur of Emperor. France has produced – it is so obvious that it hardly needs saying – some of the greatest music, art, literature, and architecture in the world. And yet even the most grateful foreigners, who have basked in all that France has given them, approach it warily.

The young Englishman James Howell, arriving in France in 1619, wrote home to his father,

> I am now in the fair Continent of France, one of Natures choicest Master-peeces; one of Ceres chiefest barns for Corn; one of Bacchus prime Wine-Cellars, and one of Neptuns best Salt-pits; a compleat self-sufficient Countrey, wher ther is rather a superfluity, then defect of anything, either for necessity or pleasure, did the policie of the Countrey correspond with Nature, in the equall distribution of the Wealth amongst the inhabitants; for I think there is not upon the earth, a richer Countrey and a poorer people.

He wrote 170 years before the fall of the Bastille.

Such abuses as he saw were improved by Time, if not by the Revolution. Yet there still remains in the foreigner an ambivalence in his attitude to the French. He is both in love with the land and puzzled by the contradictions and puzzles of the French character. No doubt this is demonstration enough of the fact that it is foolish to generalise. How can one make a remark adequate to define the race which produced both the Sun King and the Curé D'Ars, both Bardot and the Little Flower? And yet one can see that all four figures have something more than mere nationality in common. For every assertion that Frenchmen are amorous, cynical, greedy or unprincipled we could easily find 1,000 examples of abstemious, high-principled figures in every town in France. But part of the trouble seems to stem from the fact that most foreigners form their impression of France from Paris. It is a mistake which the French themselves have been making for centuries.

One of the splendid things about Charlie Waite's collection of photographs is that he is almost exclusively interested in landscape. In an earlier volume he provided us with a vision of England which no one could actually have seen since Julius Caesar's arrival in Britain in 55 BC: a depopulated island where rocks and stones and trees were apparently unthreatened by the desire of human beings to reproduce, and having reproduced to house, feed and amuse themselves. Interestingly, in his vision of France a cognate desire to blot out all vestiges of the human race has been less successful. Although France is an infinitely less crowded country than Great Britain (that is why we all swarm there each summer), it is a country which bears traces of man in almost every region. In the emptiest mountain sweep of the Pyrenees, on the most desolate tree-fringed field in the Marne, by a lake in the Vosges where you can see nothing but birches and hills and flowers, there is nevertheless this ghostlike knowledge that someone at some stage in history has been there before you.

Only in a very few places in France (in the Haute Savoie perhaps or on the more rugged snow-capped heights of the Auvergne in winter) does one ever quite feel beyond the touch or trace of one's fellow-beings: and even there, the illusion that, like Adam on the first day of creation, one is setting foot on virgin soil (or at least virgin rocks) is more often than not shattered by the cry of a goatherd or, much more likely, the sudden vision, only yards ahead, of one of those strange mountain creatures who infest all European uplands from the Italian Alps to the Trossachs: walking boots, thick socks, anoraks of bright blue or bright orange and, inevitably, a back pack. A pompom hat of some acrylic fibre usually completes the ensemble, and serves to shatter the Wordsworthian solitude.

Even without such rude interruptions to our reveries or communings with nature, there remains the strange sense in France that human beings have been there – if not forever, at least for ages. The extraordinary caves of Rouffignac in the Dordogne depict mammoths, rhinoceroses, creatures who have long since gallumped their way into extinction. Not so the human race, whose modern descendants leave less happy reminders of their existence in the picture-post-card pretty villages and valleys of the modern Dordogne, land of the *gîte* and the caravan, the pseudo-rustic inn, the converted barn with swimming pool, the expensive hovel designated a "cottage" by those who rent them out to the unsuspecting. The natives of the Dordogne seem doomed to suffer the fate of those old mammoths and obsolete pachyderms – driven out by Parisian purveyors of no-longer-nouvelle-cuisine, and by their gullible customers. The lowing of cattle and the gobbling of geese are rare sounds in the farmyards of the Dordogne – rarer by far than the strangulated English tones of middle-class "self-caterers" – too mean to stay in a hotel, and too stupid to know that "secluded cottage" in small ads means "pig-sty with no view".

I never saw the cave-paintings during my childhood or adolescence. My first intimations of ancient France came during summer holidays in Brittany whose wild Celtic landscapes (attractively reminiscent to me of South West Wales where I grew up) were full of mysterious monolithic reminders of a past age. How readily one can enter into the minds of those who, on contemplating these ancient stones, dreamed up visions of angels and devils, giants and monsters visiting the earth. The huge geological phenomena in Brittany – vast pink boulders which look as though a giantess has discarded a decorative pumice-stone from some Gargantuan boudoir – are matched by the innumerable stone reminders of mankind – menhirs, dolmens, *allées couvertes*, *pierres branlantes* and cairns.

As befits the mystic Celts, the Bretons have seen all these mysterious historic remains as vestiges of a mysterious presence. Who can ever forget their first glimpse of the Mont St Michel? Some believe it was the rock thrown by Gargantua's father as a stepping-stone when he was on his way to England to help King Arthur. But others imagine that the mount arose in more ancient times and by diabolic means. The archangel Michael, having defeated Satan, forced the fallen archangel into hard labour, erecting the mount as a stronghold of heaven against the power of hell.

Nor is it the only supernatural manifestation in Brittany. In Bourbiac, there is a stone, a vast menhir, which grew year by year like a plant until the year of Christ's Crucifixion when it stood there, complete, as a reproach to human sinfulness. At Cleder, there is a stone marked with the Devil's talons. The strange standing stones at Karnac were once an army of pagan warriors, whom St Cornely turned to stone. At Hingle, near Dinan, there is a dolmen called Pierre de Diabol, marked by the Devil himself, while at Pleleuf and at Louvigne-du-Desert there are great stones called Cadouer-an-Diol, the Devil's Chair, where he may still be seen sitting on Dark Nights.

I never saw him myself, though such stories (one hears the same kind of thing in Ireland and on the west coast of Scotland) have always had a particular charm for me, the more so, perhaps, when they are associated with places infinitely more remote and deserted. Likewise, we may believe, Ludgate Hill or Montmartre will one day be deserted promontories, where the ancient turf, undisturbed by human tread for thousands of years, is springy and abundant, and where sheep graze among a few stones and boulders. The superstitious will aver that they are the Devil's toe-nails: and who is to say that they will be altogether wrong?

How very vividly the photograph of Pointe de l'Armorique summons back teenage years on the coasts of Brittany, the extravagant geological formations, the golden sand, the wild Atlantic, all inseparable in my memory with the torment and excitement of being aged sixteen.

I was fortunate enough, in my teens, to stay with a family in Brittany. My hostess quickly discerned that the sailing-school at Perros-Guirec, and the activities of the local tennis club were less than delightful to me, and that the joke of my total incompetence wore pretty thin for those who had been partnered by me at doubles or, worse still, concussed as a result of my shy inability to shout out to the rest of the crew that I was about to *choque le foc* of my sailing-vessel. (Never having been sailing with English speakers, I do not know what this operation is called in my native language. It involves swinging the large pole at the bottom of a sail across the entire boat, knocking, when I was in control of it, everyone else on the back of the head.)

André est beaucoup plus intellectuel que sportif, Madame announced one evening over our customarily delicious dinner. With what now seems saintly dedication (I would never do the same for a charmless visiting teenager) she decreed that in future, the young members of the household would be spared my company in the afternoons, and that she would take me for drives in the countryside.

It was in this way that I first got to know the French landscape, and to develop my incipient passion for exploring antiquities. Most of the places we visited, inevitably, were churches. As in Cornwall, one learnt the names of an entire pantheon of saints quite unheard-of outside the Celtic world. From Gothic niches over primitive doorways, from wobbly old altars in decayed country churches, their dumpy little figures stared down at one – Saint Tugdual, Saint Samson, Saint Eboubibane, infinitely more important to the locals who revered them than the more mainstream dignitaries of the Roman calendar like Saint Ignatius Loyola or Saint Francis of Assisi – figures, I suspect, of whom the majority of pious Bretons had not heard – or if they had, whom they would have regarded with a certain indifference. Even in the 1960s, this strange blend of Christianity and folk-religion – so much beloved by Ernest Renan in his Breton youth – was still going strong. The crones in their elaborate lace *coifs*, the onion farmers and leather-faced fishermen, assembled summer by summer for their *pardons* – religious ceremonies which – more spontaneously than anything else dreamt up by Robespierre or George Washington – were created by the people for the people. One felt on these occasions, following some procession through a seaside town, and singing local hymns about the ability of the Virgin, with the assistance of the local Celtic saint, to provide calm seas and a good catch of lobster – that this was an entirely natural and spontaneous outburst of religious emotion. These *pardons* still happen, but the last one which I attended, with my own children, had a somewhat bogus feeling to it, as though it was being largely kept going for tourists.

One thing is certain. The Church, which used to provide a home for the naturally pious aspirations of the Bretons, is now wildly at variance with their "folk religion". The last religious ceremony which I attended in France (and I hope it really is the last) was on the Feast of the Assumption in the Cathedral at Quimper. It was being conducted by a woman in an anorak and was about as spiritually uplifting as a Social Democratic Party conference which – in ethos and tone – it strongly resembled. A man of dubious sexual predilections, attired in a modern adaptation of some monkish robes, attempted to persuade the audience or congregation to sing some appalling ditties while he accompanied them on the guitar.

The near-extinction of religion in rural France is a strange phenomenon, brought about entirely by the church authorities themselves (it has exact parallels in England and other European countries). One can drive for miles in French country districts now and find no church with its resident curé. The abolition of Christianity – yearned for so eagerly by the fathers of the revolution like Danton and Robespierre – has been carried out not by the atheist state but by the Christian Church itself.

When the older religions of our forefathers were supplanted by the Christian missionaries, the faith of the Druids and the pagans went underground, or took flight to the hills. Eventually it was to fizzle out altogether only to survive in place names, local superstitions, holy wells, standing stones. The same thing, most likely, will happen to Christianity – it is happening in our own day.

Pious people sometimes express a sort of wonderment that places such as Lourdes should flourish, while the institution of religion itself decays. In fact, the development and popularity of such manifestations is in inverse proportion to the strength of the institutional church. The more secular the bishops become, the more the faithful will look out for the numinous on their own terms. They will turn away from church – not into unbelief, but into holy places – places where, as Eliot puts it of Little Gidding, "prayer has been valid".

This partly explains the extraordinary fascination and popularity of Lourdes, the Pyrenean village where the Virgin Mary is said to have appeared to a young peasant girl, Bernadette Soubirous, and made the gnomic, not to say incomprehensible remark, "I am the Immaculate Conception." (John Betjeman used to claim that, when standing on Margate Sands, he had once had a vision of Queen Victoria floating towards him across the bobbing sea-waves, and saying, "I am the Diamond Jubilee of 1897.")

Quack cures and superstition flourished in Lourdes long before the birth of Bernadette. In the early nineteenth century, there were plenty of white witches there who claimed to possess healing power. If you failed to be cured by such a person, it was a sign that you were accursed, and special rites were enacted to purge you. Your bed, for instance, was publicly burnt – probably not a bad idea if it was riddled with the "fleas that tease in the high Pyrenees", but awkward if you did not have anywhere else to sleep. There are a lot of good old stories, about Lourdes and other places, in Mary Eyre's *A Lady Walks in the South of France in 1863*, a book which is not much read nowadays and deserves to be better known.

"When there was a storm for instance," she tells us, "all the bells in Lourdes were rung; a signal, previously agreed upon, warned the Curé to repair to the church. And will he, nill he – he was obliged to perform exorcisms, and commence a procession, whether it occurred in the night time or by day. In vain the Curés protested against the dangers of these nocturnal processions – in vain they appealed to the bishop, prejudice was too strongly rooted in the hearts of the populace and they insisted on adhering to the ancient custom."

Everything about the story of Lourdes smacks of the phoney. Yet it changes people's lives – and not merely those who go there for miraculous cures. Lourdes is not the only Pyrenean village or resort to claim visitation by the Blessed Virgin. In some regions, on both sides of the border, she would seem to have been as frequent a visitant as Queen Elizabeth I to the stately homes of England. She went to Béttharam, Héas, Sarramé and other places. The same mountains have also produced innumerable legends about pixies, fairies, elves and other supernatural presences. None of them to the modern visitor could be as magical as the mountains themselves, which *brood*. Though Maldetta is not so tall as Mont Blanc, there is something wilder and stranger about the Pyrenees than about the Alps.

"I know instances of some English valetudinarians, who have passed the winter at Aix, on the supposition that there was little or no difference between the air and the climate of Nice," wrote Tobias Smollett in one of his *Letters from France*. "This is a very great mistake which may be attended with fatal consequences. Aix is altogether exposed to the North and North-west winds, which blow as cold in Provence as ever I felt them on the mountains of Scotland."

Some of my best friends are valetudinarians of Aix, and they do not seem to have suffered from the consequences. The Northern visitor, however, who expects the South of France to provide the bland warmth of Italian seaside resorts, can be astonished by the force of the Mistral. It blows with the vigour and force of something in a myth. On the brightest of days, it suddenly comes at you, wild, cold and, quite literally, maddening. I have to stay indoors when it blows, I find myself reduced to despair by it, whereas other winds merely invigorate.

I think that if you looked at the landscape of Provence on a still, windless day, or surveyed photographs such as the ones in this book, you would still be able to tell that it was occasionally visited by this monstrous wind. I do not mean that this is simply deductible on Sherlock Holmes principles. In Charlie Waite's picture of the Mont Ste Victoire, for example, we see low-lying trees clustered and clumped. Olives in this region are more than usually gnarled. But there is more to it than that. It is something to do with the way the mountains rise, so barren and bleak out of the fertile ground.

One could believe the Mont Ste Victoire to contain some Homeric deity, his furious extended cheeks full of the wind itself. It is one of the most extraordinary mountains in the world. Cézanne's obsession with it is fully comprehensible once you see it in actuality. And those who think that Cézanne was only interested in the purely plastic qualities of mass – whether depicting naked bathers, mountains or apples – have only to visit Provence to see how deeply he was imbued with a sense of place. We appreciate his paintings all the more for seeing Provence – and yet we realise that even so great an artist is outsoared, defeated by this landscape. The whole region, stretching eastwards along the coast, through the Var and into Italy, is stunningly beautiful and – once you get a mile or two inland from the topless beaches and the villas – unspoilable, because so wild, so rugged:

Mysterious as the moons that rise.
At midnight, in the Pines of Var.

My love of France – and of the French – was strengthened when I came to write the biography of Hilaire Belloc, the poet and historian who lived from 1870 to 1953. Belloc was half French, and born at La Celle St Cloud, just outside Paris, at the time of the outbreak of the Franco-Prussian war. Because of the outcome of that war, and because his father died when Belloc was only two, the writer grew up in England, with that most useful of gifts to a writer, a sense of exile. Before going up to Balliol, Belloc did his national service in France, in the valley of the Meuse. The low-lying flat landscape, the trees reflected on grey water, the big skies depicted in the photograph of the Canal de l'Est were all familiar to him.

Thereafter, he went to France as often as he could throughout his grown-up life. When I was researching the book, I came across several of Belloc's passports which showed that he would go to France dozens of times a year. Friends remembered how, in the middle of a dinner party in London, Belloc would, on impulse, rise from the table, drain his wine-glass and ask if anyone would like to accompany him to France – in the same casual tone in which you might offer to share someone's cab to Onslow Gardens. There would then be a rush for the boat-train, and in the morning, he could put his feet on his native soil.

Belloc was a tireless walker – and talker. His friends recall rapid hikes through every region of France, Belloc shouting his head off, and his companions – younger than he – (nearly all his coevals died young for one reason or another) racing along to keep up, sometimes laughing at his absurdities, and sometimes genuinely spellbound by his intimate knowledge of the country.

Reading Belloc is like this too, and he is always at his best when he is on foot, on the move, and in France. He knew all the battles, all the poems, all the saints. Better than almost any writer in our language, he could describe *place*. Belloc was not a landscape painter. He was an historian. Wherever he rambled, usually half tight, and with a bottle of red wine sticking out of his pocket, the land itself told him a story, as in his essay on the Roman roads of Picardy:

> There is that unbroken line by which St Martin came, I think, when he rode into Amiens, and at the gate of the town cut his cloak in two to cover the beggar. It drives across country for Roye and on to Noyon, the old centre of the kings. It is a great modern road all the way, and it stretches before you mile after mile, until suddenly, without explanation and for no reason, it ends sharply, like the life of a man. It ends on the slopes of the hill called Choisy, at the edge of the wood which is there, and seek it as you will, you will never find it again . . .

Charlie Waite's camera goes beyond the point where the road stops and stories end. He recreates for us the world of the great French landscape painters. The photograph of the Miroir de Scey is strikingly like a Courbet. Unlike Mont Ste Victoire in Provence which remains unconquered by the spirit of Cézanne, we feel here as though the artist has taken over the Doubs valley and become its *genius loci*.

Ornans itself, where Courbet settled, is one of the most beautiful towns in France. It nestles in a deep valley of green rocks and vineyards. The whole town – its charming old houses and the delicate spire of the parish church are reflected in the transparent waters of the river Loue – it is all pure as the canvases of Courbet are pure. The painter's house overlooks the river. Above it, the bright green hills climb up towards the clouds which he painted so incomparably. And all around are cherry orchards – used for the manufacture of Kirsch – and vineyards.

The road journey from Ornans to Pontarlier is breathtaking, with the valley plunging deep beneath, and cascades of water pouring down from the high limestone in magnificent cataracts. It is, I believe, the only part of France where a valley is called a *Combe*, a word well-known to English and Welsh valley-dwellers.

In these pictures, we are there again. They breathe the liberating air of outdoors, the sense

Qu'il est beau d'être au monde
Et quel bien que la vie.

A.N. WILSON

LANDSCAPE IN FRANCE

AT NEUFCHÂTEL, NORTH OF REIMS, IN THE VALLEY OF THE RIVER AISNE, ARDENNES

AT CELLES SUR PLAINE, NORTH OF ST DIE, VOSGES

CHÂTEAU NEAR MARTEL, DORDOGNE

COL DU PLATZERWASEL, SOUTH WEST OF COLMAR, VOSGES

BELOW GRAND BALLON, SOUTH WEST OF COLMAR, VOSGES

SOUTH OF REMIREMONT, ALSACE LORRAINE

NEAR REMIREMONT, EAST OF FAUCOGNEY, VOSGES

MONTFORT, SOUTH OF SISTERON, PROVENCE

BELOW MONT STE VICTOIRE, PROVENCE

NEAR MONT STE VICTOIRE, PROVENCE

FORÊT BAN D'ÉTIVAL, SOUTH OF BACCARAT, VOSGES

NEAR TANCUA, FROM MOREZ, WEST OF LAUSANNE, JURA

MOUSTIERS STE MARIE, NEAR VALENSOLE, PROVENCE

CANAL DE L'EST AT LACROIX SUR MEUSE, SOUTH OF VERDUN

BETWEEN VALENSOLE AND BÉGUDE TOWARDS GORGE DE VERDON, PROVENCE

PLAN D'AUPS, AUBAGNE AREA, BOUCHES-DU-RHÔNE

LAC DE CHALAIN, EAST OF LONS-LE-SAUNIER, JURA

LAC DU MOULINET AT COMBETTES, NORTH OF MARVEJOLS, LANGUEDOC

CHAROLAIS, NEAR ST LÉGER-SOUS-BEUVRAY, BURGUNDY

STOSSWIHR, NEAR MUNSTER, WEST OF COLMAR

THE FOREST OF IRATI ON THE RIDGES BELOW THE PIC D'ORHI, PYRÉNÉES

THE RIVER DOUBS, NEAR LIÈVREMONT, NEAR PONTARLIER, DOUBS

FROM MONT VOUILLAU, ACROSS THE DOUBS VALLEY NORTH WEST OF PONTARLIER, DOUBS

FROM MONT VOUILLAU ACROSS THE DOUBS VALLEY, DOUBS

OUTSIDE MONTBRUN LES BAINS, PROVENCE

LAGRASSE, NEAR CARCASSONNE, LANGUEDOC

LAC DE LONGEMER, EAST OF GERARDMER, VOSGES

FORÊT DOMANIALE DE HEZ-FROIDMONT, DUE NORTH OF PARIS, EAST OF BEAUVAIS, OISE

MONT STE VICTOIRE, PROVENCE

LOOKING NORTH EAST FROM SALIGNAC, SOUTH OF SISTERON, PROVENCE

LAC DE REMORAY, SOUTH WEST OF PONTARLIER, DOUBS

RIVER RHÔNE, AT CULOZ, NORTH WEST OF AIX-LES-BAINS, SAVOIE

ABOVE ST CLAUDE, NORTH WEST OF LAUSANNE, JURA

NEAR MUNSTER, WEST OF COLMAR, VOSGES

NEAR FAUCOGNEY, SOUTH OF REMIREMONT, VOSGES

VIEW FROM COL DE MACEUGNE, WEST OF SISTERON, PROVENCE

NEAR MOUSTIERS, PROVENCE

CARMARGUE, PROVENCE

NEAR LE MONASTIER, ARDÈCHE

MONTBRUN NEAR MONT VENTOUX, PROVENCE

NEAR AMBOISE, LOIRE

RAON SUR PLEINE, NORTH EAST OF ST DIE, VOSGES

ON LA LANDE POURRIE, NORMANDY

BETWEEN NOYERS AND SISTERON, PROVENCE

HUNAWIHR, NEAR RIBEAUVILLE, VOSGES

CHAPEL ON THE BANKS OF LAC DE LONGEMER, EAST OF GERARDMER, VOSGES

FROM COL DE STE MARIE, EAST OF ST DIE, VOSGES

NEAR CASTELLANE, PROVENCE

FROM GRAND BALLON, SOUTH WEST OF COLMAR, VOSGES

CHÂTEAU DE VAUVENARGUES, OUTSIDE AIX-EN-PROVENCE, PROVENCE

CARMARGUE, PROVENCE

AT MENETRUX-EN-JOUS, NORTH WEST OF ST LAURENT-EN-GRANDVAUX, JURA

LA GARDE OUTSIDE CASTELLANE, PROVENCE

ALLIÈRES, NORTH WEST OF FOIX, LANGUEDOC

DORICE ON THE ESTUARY OF THE SÉE NEAR AVRANCHES, NORMANDY

CARMARGUE, PROVENCE

LAC OLZALUREKO IN THE BEECH AND PINE IRATI FOREST, PYRÉNÉES

WEST OF ST SATURNIN D'APT, PROVENCE

LA CAPELLIÈRE, CAMARGUE, PROVENCE

NEAR THANN, NORTH WEST OF MULHOUSE, VOSGES

ST TROPEZ, PROVENCE

CASSIS, PROVENCE

LE MONT ST MICHEL

NEAR DOUARNANEZ, BRITTANY

ABOVE VALS-LES-BAINS, ARDÈCHE

CHAMECHAUDE, ISÈRE, CHARTREUSE

NORTH OF GRASSE, PROVENCE

LE BILLARE, PYRÉNÉES

NORTH OF VALENCE, VERCORS

NEAR BRIANÇON, HAUTES ALPES

NEAR PÉRIGUEUX, DORDOGNE

NEAR LUCERAM, PROVENCE

ST FLORENT LE VIEIL, LOIRE

PEILLON, NEAR NICE, PROVENCE

NEAR AURILLAC, AUVERGNE

COL D'ALLOS, ALPES DE HAUTE PROVENCE

SAULIAC SUR CELÉ, LOT, DORDOGNE

BELOW MONT VENTOUX, VAUCLUSE, PROVENCE

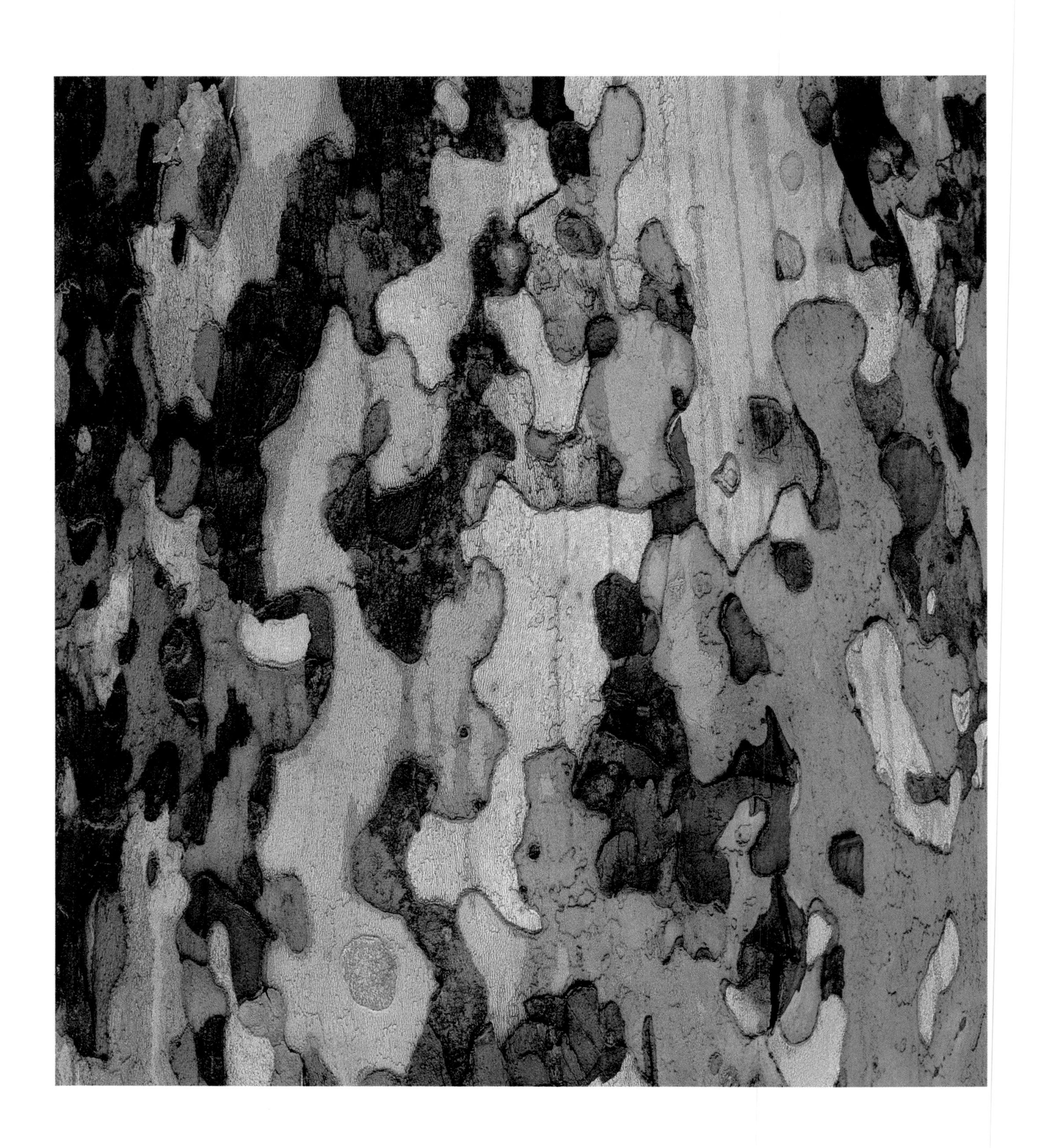

PLANE TREE, FRANCE

ALPES DE HAUTE PROVENCE

LA SALVETAT, TARN, LANGUEDOC

VENASQUE, NEAR CARPENTRAS, PROVENCE

LES GORGES DE LA BOURNE, DROME, VERCORS

TUC DE L'ETANG, PYRÉNÉES

GRANDE SÉOLANE, NEAR BARCELONNETTE, ALPES DE HAUTE PROVENCE

MOUNT GRANIER, SAVOIE, CHARTREUSE

LAC DE SERRE-PONÇON, NEAR GAP

NEAR BARCELONNETTE, ALPES DE HAUTE PROVENCE

POINTE DE L'ARMORIQUE, BRITTANY

BELOW LE POINT DE SURGATTE, NEAR ARRENS, PYRÉNÉES

CAMARGUE, PROVENCE

NEAR AUXERRE, YONNE

NEAR SATILLIEU, ARDÈCHE

COL DE PEYRESOURDE, PYRÉNÉES

GORGE D'ENGINS, ISÈRE, VERCORS

ABOVE LESCUN, PYRÉNÉES

CHAPELLE ST MARCEL, AVEYRON, AUVERGNE

CHAPELLE DES TEMPLIERS, PYRÉNÉES

CHÂTEAU SULLY, NEAR ORLÉANS, LOIRE

CANAL DE L'EST, NEAR VERDUN, ARDENNES

BETWEEN CARCASSONNE AND TRÈBES, LANGUEDOC

NEAR ST FLORENT, LOIRE

NEAR DIGNE, PROVENCE

MONT STE VICTOIRE, PROVENCE

NEAR ST JEAN PIED DE PORT, PYRÉNÉES

NEAR ST FLOUR, CANTAL, AUVERGNE

RIVER YONNE, NEAR AUXERRE

CHAMECHAUDE, ISÈRE, CHARTREUSE

NEAR BRENGUES, LOT, DORDOGNE

NEAR MURAT, CANTAL, AUVERGNE

NEAR LESCUN, PYRÉNÉES

NEAR MURAT, CANTAL, AUVERGNE

NEAR LA GRAVE, SAVOIE

PARC NATIONAL, PYRÉNÉES

LE CHEYLARD, CEVENNES

MONT DU CANTAL, AUVERGNE

COL D'ALLOS, BARCELONNETTE, ALPES DE HAUTE PROVENCE

LES AGNELIERS, ALPES DE HAUTE PROVENCE

NEAR GRAMAT, NEAR ST CÉRÉ, DORDOGNE

MONT DU CANTAL, AUVERGNE

PARC NATIONAL, NEAR LAC D'AUBERT, PYRÉNÉES

RIVER VOLANE, NEAR ANTRAIGUES, ARDÈCHE

NEAR LARRAU, PYRÉNÉES

NEAR CHORGES, HAUTES ALPES

NEAR JAUSIERS, ALPES DE HAUTE PROVENCE

NEAR CONDOM, GARONNE

NEAR MARTEL, DORDOGNE

MONT STE VICTOIRE, PROVENCE

RIVER ARDÈCHE, BALAZUC

RIVER VEZÈRE AT UZERCHE, DORDOGNE

NEAR PAS DE PEYROL, CANTAL, AUVERGNE

LAC DE THORENC, VAR, PROVENCE

RIVER ISÈRE, DROME

NEAR ST CLAUDE VALFIN, JURA

MIROIR DE SCEY, SOUTH OF BESANÇON, DOUBS

NEAR GIRONS, PYRÉNÉES

PONT EN ROYANS, DROME, VERCORS

NEAR ST BÉAT, PYRÉNÉES

ABOVE GARIN, PYRÉNÉES

BRANTES, BELOW MONT VENTOUX, PROVENCE

NEAR BANNALEC, FINISTÈRE